Talent Show
Scaredy-Pants

Ready, Freddy!

Talent Show Scaredy-Pants

by ABBY KLEIN

illustrated by
JOHN MCKINLEY

SCHOLASTIC INC.
New York   Toronto   London   Auckland   Sydney
Mexico City   New Delhi   Hong Kong   Buenos Aires

EX. 68107

To the best grandparents in the world:
Papa Bob, Grammy Audrey,
Papa Harry, and Grammy Shirley.
I love you with all my heart!
—A. K.

THE BLUE SKY PRESS

Text copyright © 2005 by Abby Klein
Illustrations copyright © 2005 by John McKinley
All rights reserved.

Special thanks to Robert Martin Staenberg.

Library of Congress catalog card number: 2004016683
ISBN 0-439-55604-X
10 9 8 7   06 07 08 09
Printed in the United States of America   23
First printing, May 2005

CHAPTERS

I have a problem.

A really, really, big problem.

My class is having a talent

show, and I have no talent!

Let me tell you about it.

CHAPTER 1

Ladies and Gentlemen

"OK, listen, everyone," said my teacher, Mrs. Wushy. "Next Monday is Grandparents' Day here at school. Your grandparents are invited to spend the whole day with us."

Robbie raised his hand. "Excuse me, Mrs. Wushy, but my grandparents don't live around here."

"Yeah, and I don't have any grandparents," Max butted in.

"That's OK, boys," Mrs. Wushy said. "You can borrow a grandparent for the day, like a neighbor or a family friend. I do hope you bring somebody, though, because I thought it would be fun to put on a talent show for all our special guests."

I raised my hand.

"Yes, Freddy," said Mrs. Wushy.

"You mean put on a show in front of *all* the grandparents?"

"Of course that's what she means, silly," said Chloe, fluffing her strawberry-blonde curls and smiling her biggest movie-star smile. "We are going to be the stars!"

I gulped. "I don't think that's such a good idea," I said, as my stomach started to do flip-flops.

"Why not?" asked Jessie.

"Yeah, why not?" Max butted in again. "Does the little baby have stage fright?"

"Noooo," I started to protest, but then Mrs. Wushy cut me off.

"All right. Enough, Max. Don't worry, Freddy. I promise you'll have a great time. I do this every year, and the grandparents love it. Now I will need everyone to think of an act for the show. Does anyone have any ideas?"

Chloe's hand shot up. As soon as Mrs. Wushy called on her, she leaped to her feet and started doing some kind of ballet moves. "I could do the 'Dance of the Sugarplum Fairy' from *The Nutcracker*," she said, twirling. "I'm really good at it because I've been practicing in my ballet class. I even have the outfit to go with it. It has fairy wings, and a tiara, and a tutu decorated with candies, and . . ."

"She's such a show-off," I whispered to

my best friend, Robbie. "I wish she would sit down already and be quiet!"

Just then, Max grabbed her by the arm and said, "OK, little Miss Priss, you can stop bragging and sit down now," as he pulled her back down to the rug.

"OWWWW! Let me go! Mrs. Wushy, did you see what he did?" Chloe said, folding her arms across her chest and pouting. "I was just showing you my talent."

"Max, you need to keep your hands to yourself. What do you say to Chloe?"

"Sorry," he mumbled.

"What? I can't hear you," Chloe sneered, cupping her ear with her hand. "You know an apology doesn't count unless you can hear the person say it."

"Sorry!" Max yelled in her ear.

"All right, you two," Mrs. Wushy said.

"Please go sit on opposite ends of the rug.
Does anyone else have ideas for the show?"

Jessie raised her hand.

"Yes, Jessie."

"I could do flamenco."

"Flamingo?" said Max, chuckling. "Are you gonna dress up like a bird?"

"For your information, Mister, flamenco is a type of Spanish dance. I've been learning it from my *abuela*, my grandma, who lives with me and my mom. She has been teaching it to me after school. It's sort of tricky, but I think I'm good enough to do it in the show."

"That sounds cool," I said. "I bet you're really good."

"Thanks, Freddy," Jessie said, smiling.

"Hey, I'm good, too," Chloe whined. "Why didn't you say that to me?"

"Because you're so annoying, you little brat," Max snapped.

"What did you say?" Chloe asked. She glared at Max.

"That's it!" said Mrs. Wushy. "Come sit in these chairs, and I don't want to hear

15

another word from either of you, or you'll both be going to have a little chat with Mr. Pendergast."

"Uh-oh," I whispered to Robbie. Mr. Pendergast is our principal. We call him The Skunk because his breath stinks.

"That sounds like a great idea, Jessie," said Mrs. Wushy. "I love flamenco dancing, and that's a wonderful way to share some of your culture. Any other ideas?"

Kids kept raising their hands, and everyone had an idea for the talent show. Everyone except me. I had no talent. What was I going to do? I couldn't even whistle!

"OK, I think I've got all of you on my list," said Mrs. Wushy, "except you, Freddy. What would you like to do?"

"I don't know," I mumbled, shrugging my shoulders.

"I'm sure you're good at lots of things. How about singing a song? You love sharks, right? Why don't you sing a song about sharks? I'm sure you know one."

Was she crazy? I don't even sound good when I sing in the shower! I wasn't about to sing in front of everyone's grandparents! "No, I'm not a very good singer."

"How about telling jokes?"

"Nah, I don't know any funny ones."

"Do you play an instrument?"

"Nope." Mrs. Wushy was getting a little frustrated, but I can't help it if I'm a loser— a loser with no talent.

"Well, why don't you think about it tonight and tell me tomorrow."

"OK, sure," I said, but more time wasn't going to help me unless someone had a magic spell for talent.

CHAPTER 2

Loser!

When we got on the bus to go home, I plopped myself down next to Robbie, leaned my head back against the seat, and let out a giant sigh. I had to come up with something to do for the talent show. I hit my forehead with the palm of my hand. "Think, think, think."

"Don't worry, Freddy. You'll come up with something to do for the show," Robbie said. "You're good at lots of things."

"Oh yeah? Name one."

"You're the best dodgeball player ever in the history of Lincoln Elementary."

"Great! And what do you suggest I do for the show? Have all the grandparents throw balls at me while I jump around the stage trying not to get hit?"

"OK, well, you're really good at catching bugs. You could catch some really cool bugs and bring them in," Robbie said.

"Oh, I can see it now. . . . Everyone's grandma screaming while I hold up a big, fat, juicy earthworm and say, 'Just look at this beauty I caught yesterday.'"

"Oh, I know," Robbie interrupted. "You're a shark expert. You could do a really cool skit about sharks and . . ."

"Face it, Robbie," I said, cutting him off. "I can't do anything. I'm just a loser."

I leaned my head back against the seat again and closed my eyes.

"Freddy is a loser! Freddy is a loser!"

Oh no! Was I hearing what I thought I was hearing? Was Max, the biggest bully in all of first grade, telling the whole bus that I was a loser? I opened my eyes. Yep. There was Max, with his hands cupped around his mouth, chanting, "Freddy is a loser! Freddy is a loser!"

"Shut up, Max!" I muttered angrily under my breath.

"Did you say something?" Max asked, whipping his head around in my direction.

"Who, me?" I asked, shrinking back down into my seat.

"Yeah, you," he said, poking his finger into my chest.

"Uh, I just said, 'I give up, Max.'"

"That's what I thought, Loser," he said.

I rubbed my chest where he had poked it, as he slid back down into his seat.

Robbie grabbed my arm and whispered, "Don't let him get to you."

"I can't help it," I said. I sat there staring

at the back of Max's head. "Stupid, dumb, dumb, Poopyhead," I mumbled.

"What was that, Loser?" Max asked, jumping up and grabbing me by the shirt.

Boy, this guy must have some kind of supersonic hearing. I gulped. "I said, 'Oh, I wished I'd stayed in bed.'"

"That's not what it sounded like," Max said, tightening his grip on my shirt. Soon I wouldn't be able to breathe.

"Well, that's what I heard," said Robbie. "And I'm sitting right next to him."

I owed Robbie big-time. I think he just saved my life.

"Are you sure?" Max asked.

"Yep," Robbie answered, nodding his head.

"If you say so," said Max, loosening his grip on my shirt.

Max gave me the evil eye and sat back down. I turned to Robbie and whispered, "I owe you one."

"No you don't," he whispered back. "That's what friends are for."

CHAPTER 3

Can You Make Me Disappear?

"Freddy, you know Grandparents' Day is only a week away," my mom said that night at dinner. "I spoke to Papa Dave and Grammy Rose today, and they can't wait to come to school with you."

"Well, they shouldn't get too excited," I said. "In fact, they may not even want to come at all. I think it's actually going to be pretty boring."

"No it's not," my big sister Suzie chimed in. "I remember when I was in first grade, and we had Grandparents' Day. It was really fun! Papa and Grammy get to sit on the rug with you and eat lunch with you in the cafeteria. The best part is the talent show."

"What talent show?" my dad asked.

"The kids put on a talent show for all the grandparents. Don't you remember I sang 'Over the Rainbow,' and all the grandparents started to cry?"

"Oh, I remember," my mom said. "Grammy Rose said you stole the show. You were the star!"

"You were the star. You were the star," I muttered under my breath. "I think I'm gonna puke."

"So, Freddy, what are you going to do for the talent show?" my mom asked.

I shrugged my shoulders. "I dunno," I mumbled into my shirt.

"Did Mrs. Wushy have the sign-ups yet?" Suzie asked.

I wished the Big Mouth would just mind her own business. "Yeah, today."

"So let me guess," said my mom. "You signed up to sing, too. Just like Suzie did."

To sing? Was she crazy? "I can't sing, Mom," I said.

"What do you mean you can't sing? I hear you every night in the shower, singing your heart out. 'She'll be comin' round the mountain when she comes. Toot, toot.'"

"That's in the shower. Not in front of a whole group of people! I would die before I'd get up and sing in front of a whole group of people."

"No, I know. He signed up to juggle," said my dad.

Juggle? Didn't these people know anything? "Dad, don't you remember the last time I tried juggling? I almost killed poor Mako."

"You did?"

"Yeah. I was practicing with oranges in my room, and I dropped one by accident. It landed in Mako's fishbowl and nearly squished him to death."

"You had oranges in your room?" my mom butted in. "You know you're not allowed to have food in your room."

"I wasn't eating them. I was using them

to practice juggling. Besides, Dad was there. He said it was OK."

My mom glared at my dad. "You did, Daniel? Why didn't you tell me?"

"Oh, honey, don't get all worked up," my dad said.

"But rules are rules, and I really don't appreciate it when you change them behind my back like that."

"Can we have this discussion later?" my dad said, as he turned back to me. "Right now, I'd like to hear what Freddy signed up to do for the show."

"Yeah. Me, too!" said my sister.

I wished she would just stay out of this! "I already told you guys. I didn't sign up for anything yet!"

"Well, you must have signed up for *something*," said my mom.

"No, I didn't."

"What did Mrs. Wushy say?" Suzie asked.

"None of your beeswax," I said.

"Freddy, don't talk to your sister that way," said my mom. "She just asked you a question. What *did* Mrs. Wushy say?"

"She said I could tell her tomorrow."

"We'll help you think of something by then," said my dad.

"Good luck," I said, "because I'm just a loser with no talent."

"You got that right," Suzie said, laughing.

"Suzie," said my mom, "that is not nice to say. Freddy is a very talented young man."

"Well, you're wrong about that," I said, "unless someone in this family has some magic spell for talent."

"Hey, you just gave me a great idea," my dad said.

CHAPTER 4

A Little Magic

"Remember that magic set Papa Dave got Suzie for her birthday?" my dad asked.

"Yeah," I said slowly, thinking he might be on to something.

"I could teach you how to do a couple of tricks, and then you could do them for the talent show. How about that?"

"Hey, that's *my* set that Papa Dave got for *me*!" Suzie whined.

"You can't share it with your brother?" my mom asked.

"What if he loses some of the pieces?"

"I won't lose the pieces," I said.

"Oh yeah? You lose my stuff all the time."

"Do not."

"Do too."

"Do not."

"Do too."

"Stop it right now, you two," my mother said, clapping her hands loudly. "Suzie, you can share the set with your brother."

"But . . ."

"No 'buts,'" said my dad. "Freddy can use it, and if he loses any pieces, then I will get you a new one. Now please go get it."

"Fine," she answered and left the room in a huff.

I was starting to get excited. Doing magic tricks was actually a really good idea. No one else in the class had signed up to do that.

"I didn't even know you knew how to do magic, Dad," I said.

"Papa Dave taught me how to do a bunch of tricks when I was your age. I used to put on little magic shows for the kids in my neighborhood. They called me Daniel the Great."

Wow! I was really beginning to like this idea. Freddy the Great sure sounded a lot better than Freddy the Loser. Just then, Suzie came back with the magic set and thrust the box into my chest so hard I almost fell over.

"Here you go, Fathead. You'd better not lose any of the pieces, or you'll be sorry," she said, wagging her finger in my face.

"Suuuuzie," my dad said, "get your finger out of your brother's face. You're going to poke him in the eye. He's not going to lose any of the pieces, and if you can't share your toys with Freddy, then maybe we should just stop buying you toys altogether."

"THAT'S NOT FAIR!" Suzie protested. Her hands were on her hips, and she stomped the ground with her foot.

"Don't you raise your voice at me, young

36

lady," my dad said. "Now go to your room until you calm down. Don't come out until you can talk like a normal person."

"NO! NO! NO!" she wailed. "I'm not going!"

"Oh, yes you are," my mom said, taking her by the arm and pulling her out of the room still screaming.

"Hey, Dad, can you teach me that trick?" I said. "Making Suzie disappear?"

"Freeeddy," my dad said, trying not to laugh. But I could see he thought what I said was funny. "Come on, let's look at the instruction book. This set has 150 different tricks. I'm sure we can find some that will really wow your friends."

On the cover of the book was a picture of a kid dressed as a magician, pulling a rabbit out of a hat. "Hey, Dad. Can you teach me how to do that?"

"Do what?"

"Pull a rabbit out of a hat?"

"Of course. Any good magician knows how to do that," said my dad. "It's actually a pretty easy trick, and the set even comes with a stuffed rabbit you can use."

"That would be great!" I said. I could just see my friends' faces now. Their mouths would be hanging open, and all the grand-parents would be clapping wildly. Just like Suzie, I would be the star of the talent show.

My dad waved his hand in front of my face. "Earth to Freddy. Earth to Freddy. Are you listening to me?"

"Oh, yeah, sorry, Dad."

"All you need for the trick is this special top hat and the stuffed rabbit."

"Okey dokey."

"You see," my dad continued, "the hat has a fake bottom. The audience thinks they're looking at the bottom of the hat, but there is actually a little flap that lifts up where you can hide the rabbit underneath."

"Cool," I said.

"Before the trick starts, when no one is looking, you hide the rabbit under the flap like this." My dad lifted up the flap and hid the rabbit. "See, you can't tell that anything is under there."

I grabbed the hat from him. It looked just like a regular old hat. "This trick's going to be great!"

"Now watch carefully, and I'll show you how it's done. You hold the hat by the brim with the flap facing toward you. Show the audience that the hat is empty by tilting it just a little. Then you wave your magic wand over the hat and say, 'Abracadabra, I will now pull a rabbit out of my hat.' Take the hat in your other hand so that the flap is on the opposite side and falls open. Then pull the rabbit out."

"That is awesome, Dad! You're a genius!" I said, hugging him.

"OK, now you try it, Freddy."

I grabbed the hat from him.

"Remember," my dad said, "the first time the flap faces toward you, and the second time it faces away from you."

"Yeah, yeah, I think I got it," I said. I cleared my throat. "Hmph, hmph. Ladies and gentlemen, Freddy the Great will now pull a rabbit out of a hat. Watch closely. As you can see, there is no rabbit in this hat." I tipped the hat toward my dad. "Abracadabra, I will now pull a rabbit out of my hat." I waved the wand over the hat, put the hat in my other hand so that the

flap would fall open, and pulled the rabbit out. "Tah-dah!"

"That was great, Freddy!" my dad said. "You're a natural."

"Let's do another one!"

Just then my mom walked in the room. "OK, you two. It's getting late. You'll have to practice some more tricks tomorrow."

"Please, Mom, just one more."

"No, it's past your bedtime, and you've got school tomorrow. Go upstairs to brush and wash, and I'll be up in a minute."

"Oh, all right. I'm going." As I climbed the stairs, I thought maybe someday I could get good enough to magically change the time on the clock so I could go to bed whenever I wanted. But I wasn't good enough. At least not yet!

CHAPTER 5

Is that
a Real Rabbit?

The next morning, I raced to the bus stop. I couldn't wait to tell everyone what I was going to do for the talent show. Overnight, Freddy the Loser had magically become Freddy the Great. When the bus pulled up, I leaped up the steps and walked right past Max with my head held high.

"Look who's here," Max said, chuckling.

"It's the loser. Hey, Freddy, I think I see a big L on your forehead." He held up his thumb and pointer finger in the shape of an L.

"Well, then maybe you need glasses, Max, because I am no longer a loser," I said as I sat down next to Robbie.

"Oh no?" snorted Max.

"Nope," I answered. "From now on, you can just call me Freddy the Great."

"OK, Freddy the Great Big Wimp."

I ignored his stupid comment and kept on talking. "I have a really cool act for the class talent show."

"Oh really?" Max said, raising his eyebrows. "Let me guess. Instead of making animals out of balloons, you're going to make animals out of all your boogers."

Some kids started laughing hysterically. I wanted to cry, but I held back the tears and took a deep breath. I was not going to let Max get to me today. I was Freddy the Great.

"Nope. Wrong again. I'm going to do a little magic. *I* am going to pull a rabbit out of my hat," I said as I pretended to pull an imaginary rabbit out of my baseball cap.

"You are?" Max asked.

"Yes, I am."

"A real, live rabbit?"

"Well, umm . . ." I stammered.

"I knew it!" Max yelled. "What is it? Your little stuffed bunny?"

"Actually, it belongs to my sister, Suzie," I mumbled.

"Isn't that cute," Max teased. "Little baby

Fweddy is going to pway wif his stuffed bunny wunny."

My face turned bright red. I slid way down in my seat. I wished I could make myself disappear.

"Come on. Just ignore him, Freddy," Robbie whispered. "I think doing magic tricks is a really great idea."

"Thanks, Robbie," I said and sighed as I slipped farther down in the seat. "It *would* be pretty cool if I had a real rabbit to use. Too bad you don't have a little white rabbit. You have a leopard gecko and a ball python, but no rabbit!"

"Don't forget about my mouse, Cheesy. Maybe you could use *him*. He's small and soft and furry, just like a rabbit."

"Are you serious? You'd let me borrow

Cheesy for the talent show?" I asked, sitting up a bit straighter.

"Sure, why not? It's not like you're really going to make him disappear forever. It's just an illusion. Right?"

"Yeah, right. Can you bring him over to my house after school today, and we can do a little rehearsal?"

"But your mom doesn't like animals in the house," Robbie said.

"She doesn't. We'll have to sneak him in. That shouldn't be too hard. After all, he's small enough to fit in your pocket." I threw my arms around Robbie. "You're the best friend in the whole world. Thanks. What would I do without you?"

"Let's hope we don't ever have to find out," Robbie answered with a smile.

CHAPTER 6

Mouse Magic

"I'll get it!" I yelled as I bounded down the stairs to answer the door. It was Robbie and Cheesy, and I didn't want my mom anywhere near that mouse. If she knew I was bringing a mouse into the house, she would freak out! She thinks pets are smelly and dirty. Our house is so clean, even a mouse wouldn't be able to find a crumb on the floor.

"Don't open the door until you ask who

it is," my mom called from her office in the back of the house.

"OK, Mom!" I yelled back. "Robbie, is that you?" I asked from my side of the door.

"Yeah. It's me."

I flung open the door and went to give Robbie a hug. "Did you bring him?" I asked anxiously.

"Be careful. You're going to squish him. He's right in here," he said, pulling his jacket pocket open so I could see inside.

"Hey, Cheesy," I whispered, peering into Robbie's pocket. "Thanks for helping me out, little guy."

"Sure, Freddy. Anytime," Robbie squeaked.

"OK, Robbie," I said, grabbing his arm. "Let's get to my room before my mom sees Cheesy and has a hissy fit."

We ran upstairs to my room and slammed

the door closed. I didn't want to take a chance of Cheesy escaping. "This will be so awesome if it works," I said to Robbie. "Max will never call me a loser again. I really will be Freddy the Great."

Robbie pulled Cheesy out of his pocket and lifted him up to his face. "OK, Cheeseball, are you ready to be Freddy's special assistant?"

I went to my closet to get the magic hat and brought it back to Robbie. "You see? The hat has a fake bottom," I said, lifting up the flap. "I just need to hide Cheesy in this secret place underneath until it's time to pull him out. I think he'll fit."

"Let's see," Robbie said, gently placing Cheesy into the secret hole and pulling the flap over him.

"He fits perfectly," I said, jumping up and down and clapping my hands. "Now go sit down over there," I said, pointing to my bed, "and I'll do the trick for you."

Robbie walked over and flopped down on my bed.

"Ladies and gentlemen," I began. "Here in my hands, I have an empty hat." I tilted the hat toward Robbie and waved my wand around the inside. "As you can see, there is nothing inside. Now, watch, and be amazed. Let me say the magic words. Abracadabra," I continued, waving the wand in a circular motion around the hat, "and . . ." I reached inside and pulled Cheesy out. "Tah-dah!"

"Wow, Freddy! That was awesome," Robbie said excitedly. "You looked just like those magicians I see on TV."

"This trick is going to be great!" I said, smiling. "Robbie, you're the best."

Just as I thought everything was finally going my way, Suzie burst into the room. "Hey, Booger Breath, where's my new Superstars CD?" she barked. "I told you not to take it!"

The noise scared Cheesy, who jumped out of my hands and scurried out the door.

CHAPTER 7

Stop that Mouse!

"AHHHHHHHH! There's a mouse in the house!" Suzie screamed as she jumped up on my bed.

"Cheesy, Cheesy, come back!" Robbie called, dropping to his hands and knees and scurrying after him.

I ran over to the bed and covered Suzie's mouth with my hand. "Shhhhhh," I said. "It's just Cheesy, Robbie's pet mouse."

"You will be grounded for *life* if Mom sees that disgusting thing," she said through my hand.

"He's not disgusting. He's cute. Now are you going to help us catch him or not?"

"First, get your hand off my mouth."

I dropped my hand.

"What's in it for me?" Suzie asked.

"I don't know. . . . I'll let you be the boss of the remote control for a week."

"Wow! You must really want my help," said Suzie. "Fine. It's a deal," she said, and we locked pinkies. "Pinkie swear?" she asked, staring me down.

"Pinkie swear," I said. "Now let's get going before he goes downstairs. Remember: Act casual if you see Mom. We don't want her to know what we're looking for."

We got down on all fours and scrambled after Robbie, who was searching the bathroom. We looked under my shark pajamas lying on the floor. No Cheesy. We looked in my pile of super-shark bath toys. No Cheesy. We even looked through my dirty underwear in the hamper. No Cheesy.

Catching a mouse was harder than I thought. It's so tiny that it can hide almost

anywhere, and it's not like a dog that comes running when you call it. Cheesy wasn't in the bathroom, so we looked in Suzie's room, my parents' room, and their bathroom. Nothing. I guess that saying "quiet as a mouse" is really true.

"Where can he be?" I groaned. "If we don't find him, my life is over."

Then I heard it.

"AHHHHHHH!!!" My mom's scream probably cracked every mirror in the house.

"Oh no! She found Cheesy!"

"Well, it's been nice knowing you," Suzie said, patting me on the back.

We all ran downstairs to the kitchen. We found my mom, but there was no Cheesy anywhere in sight.

"Mom, are you all right?" I asked.

"Oh, yes. Sorry if I scared you, kids. I just burned this batch of cookies for the talent show. You kids just go back to whatever you were playing."

Whew. That was a close one. I couldn't believe my luck. My life had been spared. But this meant that Cheesy was still loose in the house. I grabbed Robbie and yanked him into the dining room. "Where does Cheesy like to hide?" I whispered.

"I don't know. I usually don't let him run around loose."

We started to crawl into the living room when we heard it again.

"AHHHHHHH!"

"I wonder what she burned this time," I said.

We ran back to the kitchen, and this time we found my mom crouched on top of the kitchen table with a big broom in her hand.

"HELP!!! HELP!!!" she screamed. "THERE'S A MOUSE IN THE HOUSE!"

"The broom!" Robbie gasped. "What's she doing with the broom?"

I knew I would be in the biggest trouble of my life if I told my mom I brought a mouse into the house, but I couldn't let my mom hit poor little Cheesy over the head with a broom.

"MOM! WAIT!" I yelled.

"KIDS, STAND BACK! THERE'S A MOUSE IN THE HOUSE!" she screamed. She had this crazy look in her eyes, and she was breathing really fast.

"Hey, there he goes!" Robbie called as Cheesy scampered across the kitchen floor, heading toward the stove.

"DON'T TOUCH IT!" my mom shouted. "IT HAS GERMS!"

Robbie dove after Cheesy and caught him, just as Cheesy was about to run right under the stove.

"PUT THAT DOWN! PUT THAT DOWN!"
my mom yelled, panting.

"It's OK, Mrs. Thresher," Robbie said,
holding Cheesy in the palm of his hand.
"He belongs to me."

"He wha-aaat?" she stammered.

"He belongs to me. He's my pet mouse,
Cheesy. He's harmless."

My mom slowly climbed down off the kitchen table.

"Well, I guess we found him," I said.

"Freddy, what in the world is going on here?" my mom asked. "I demand an explanation right this minute!"

"This should be good," Suzie muttered under her breath.

"I . . . well, you see . . . I . . . ummm," I stammered.

"Freddy Alan Thresher, if you don't answer me this instant, then you will be punished like you've never been punished before. I am not playing games."

I burst into tears. "I'm sorry, Mom," I sobbed. "It's just that . . . Max . . . I'm a loser . . . no talent . . . magic . . . with a mouse . . . Freddy the Great . . ."

"Freddy, you need to stop crying and take a deep breath. I can't understand a word you're saying."

"Um, Mrs. Thresher, may I please say something?" Robbie asked.

"Of course, Robbie."

"Max has been teasing Freddy an awful lot lately, so Freddy thought Max might leave him alone if he did a really cool magic trick at the talent show."

"Yeah, Mom," I said, sniffling. "I wanted to pull a real rabbit out of a hat, but I don't have a real rabbit, so I asked Robbie if I could borrow Cheesy. Please don't be mad, Mom. I wanted Max to think I was Freddy the Great, not Freddy the Loser."

"Oh, Freddy," my mom said, pulling me onto her lap and giving me a hug. "You are

not a loser. To me, you will always be Freddy the Great."

"You mean you're not going to punish him?" Suzie asked.

I glared at Suzie and mouthed the words, "Thanks a lot!"

"I didn't say that," my mom continued. "Freddy, I am still angry about the fact that you went behind my back and brought an animal into the house without asking me first."

"I know, Mom. I'm sorry. I promise I won't ever do it again."

"That's it?" Suzie whined. "He doesn't get any consequences?"

"Are you his mother? Last time I checked, you were his sister, not his mother," my mom said. "This is not your business."

"But . . ."

"One more word from you, Suzie, and *you* will be punished."

Suzie turned and stomped off in a huff. "The deal's off!" I called after her.

"Come on, Robbie, I'll take you and Cheesy home," my mom said. "And do me a favor. Don't ever bring him into this house again!"

CHAPTER 8

Grandpa
the Great

I did lose my TV privileges for two weeks because I had a mouse in the house. And I had to promise my parents that I would not do a trick that involved any kind of live animals.

"Well, I'm not going to use that stupid stuffed bunny," I told my dad. "So now I have no act for the show. Thanks a lot!"

"Now, Freddy, that's not true. There are other tricks you can do," my dad said.

"Oh yeah? Like what?"

"You know what I think you need?"

"What?" I asked.

"You need the Magic Man himself."

"Who?"

"Papa Dave. He knows all the coolest tricks. Let's call him and see if he can come over tomorrow and teach you a couple of his best tricks."

My dad called my grandpa, and Papa Dave agreed to come over and teach me some of his coolest tricks.

The next day, Papa Dave arrived at the house wearing a black cape and hat and carrying a big bag of tricks.

"Hey, Sport," he said, picking me up. "How about you and I do a little magic?"

"Can you make me invisible, so I don't have to be in the talent show on Monday?"

"Come on, now, Freddy. You wouldn't want to disappoint your grammy now, would you? She expects you to be the star of the show!"

"She does?"

"Yep. So come on over here, and let's look at my little book of magic. I'll teach you how to do any trick you want."

I flipped through the pages of the book and stopped at a trick called "Pin-Through-the-Thumb." If you do it right, it looks as if you're sticking a pin right through your thumb. "Wow. This one looks pretty cool, Papa."

"This is one of my favorites, Kiddo. And I promise, if you do this trick, that kid Max

72

you were telling me about won't call you a
baby anymore."

"Really, Papa? Can you teach it to me? Is
it hard to do?"

"Nah. All you have to do is cut a piece of potato the size of your thumb. Then you hold the potato in your left hand, hide your whole hand under a handkerchief, and act like the potato is your real thumb. You say, 'Ladies and gentlemen, watch closely. I will now stick a pin through my thumb.' Then you jam the pin into your fake thumb. That will get a lot of oohs and aahs from the audience."

"Awesome."

"What other tricks would you like to learn?" Papa Dave asked. "I can teach you any ones you want."

We spent the afternoon picking out the best magic tricks and practicing them. Papa Dave taught me how to do the "Torn Newspaper," where you rip up a piece of newspaper and then magically put it back together; the "Linking Rings," where three solid rings are linked together and then pulled apart; and the "Magic Card," where the number of diamonds on the card appears to change each time you turn the card over.

"Now, let's see. You need one last trick for the grand finale."

Just then, Suzie walked in. "Hey, can you teach me how to make her disappear?"

"That's not funny." Suzie scowled at me.

"No, I can't do that," said Papa Dave, "but maybe she can be your assistant for the grand finale."

"What?!" Suzie protested. "Why should I help the little Poophead?"

"Because he's your brother, and you love

him very much," Papa Dave said, winking at her. "How 'bout it, sweetie?"

"What do I have to do?"

"Freddy is going to do this 'Ghost Wand' trick. The audience will think a ghost is making his wand tap on the table. He will set the wand down between two candlesticks, and when he says the magic words, you will secretly pull on this clear string that is strung between the two candlesticks. It will look as if the wand is tapping on the table without anyone holding it!"

"Wow! That'll really blow everyone away!" I said excitedly. "What do you think, Suzie?"

"It is pretty cool," she said. "Can I wear a special outfit for the show?"

"If you help me, you can wear anything you want," I said.

"Then I'll do it."

"Suzie, you're the best sister in the whole world."

"I know," she said, smiling.

"Great! Then we're all set," said Papa Dave. "Freddy the Great, you are going to be the star of the show!"

CHAPTER 9

The Big Show

The big day finally came, and all the kids were really excited.

Chloe twirled around on her tiptoes and boasted, "Look how beautiful I am! My grandma says I'm going to be the star of the whole show."

"Not today," Papa Dave whispered in my ear. "Not today."

Just then Jessie came over with her grandma. *"Abuela, ¿te acuerdas de mi amigo,*

Freddy? Freddy, remember my grandma, Maria, who lives with me?"

"Of course. She makes the best tamales in the whole world! *Hola*," I said, waving. "This is my Papa Dave and my Grammy Rose. Sorry, they don't speak Spanish."

"*Mucho gusto*," Papa Dave said, shaking Maria's hand.

"Papa, I didn't know you speak Spanish."

"*Un poquito*," he said, smiling.

We all went to sit down. "That Jessie sure is cute, Freddy," my grandma said.

"That's his girlfriend," Suzie teased.

"She is not. She's just my friend."

"Well, then why are you turning red, Loverboy?" Suzie continued.

"Shut up!" I snapped.

"Enough, you two," said my grandma.

"Suzie, please leave him alone. This is Freddy's special day."

As we took our seats, I noticed that Max was sitting all by himself. I remembered he didn't have grandparents. I knew his parents were both at work, and he didn't see his dad very much, but what about a neighbor or a grown-up friend?

"Oh, look. That boy over there is sitting all by himself," my grammy said. "Freddy, why don't you see if he wants to come over here and sit by us?"

Was she kidding? Ask Max, the biggest bully in all of first grade, the one who makes my life miserable, to sit with us? "I think he's OK over there," I said.

"No one should really be without a grandparent on Grandparents' Day, Freddy.

Come on, go ask him," said Papa Dave, gently pushing me in Max's direction.

"But, Papa . . . that's Max."

"*The* Max?"

"Yep. The one and only."

"Oh. I see. Well, just because he's mean and nasty doesn't mean that you have to be. Come on. Go ask him. Kill him with kindness, like I always say."

Reluctantly, I got up and walked over to where Max was sitting.

"Yeah? What do *you* want, Loser?" Max mumbled without looking up.

"I . . . uh . . . I was wondering if you wanted to come sit with me and my papa and grammy."

"Ha, ha, very funny, but I'm not in the mood for jokes right now," Max said.

All of a sudden, I felt sorry for him. He seemed really sad. "No, I mean it. I'm not kidding. Why don't you come over and sit with us? You can pretend that my grand-parents are your grandparents today."

He looked up. "You mean it?" he asked.

"Yeah. Come on."

The two of us walked over to where Suzie and my grandparents were sitting. "Well,

this must be Max," Papa Dave said. "Nice to meet you, Max. How would you like to be my grandson for today?"

I couldn't believe it. I think I actually saw Max smile.

"Uh, yeah. Sure. Thanks," he said, sitting down next to us.

"You really are Freddy the Great," my papa whispered in my ear. "I love you."

Just then Mrs. Wushy said, "OK, everyone, please sit down. I'd like to welcome you all to Room 3's annual Grandparents' Day Talent Show. We certainly have a talented group of children here. I know you're really going to enjoy yourselves. First, I'd like to introduce Max Sellars, who will play the bongos for you."

"Yeah, Max," my papa yelled out. "Show 'em what you've got!"

Wow! I was shocked! Max was actually a really good bongo player. When he was finished, everyone clapped wildly.

"That was great, Max," my papa said.

"Uh, thanks," he said, as his lips curled slightly at the corners.

Next Chloe went, and I'm happy to say

she fell right on her butt. Serves her right for all that bragging.

Jessie did the flamenco like a pro, and she did look pretty in her ruffled dress. "*¡Bravo, bravo, mi muñeca!*" her grandma called, tossing a flower onto the stage.

Robbie walked out onstage wearing one of those funny things that makes you look like you have an arrow through your head. Then he told some really funny jokes. I think my favorite one was "Why did Tigger stick his head in the toilet? Because he was looking for Pooh."

Eventually it was my turn.

"And now Freddy Thresher will perform some magic for us," Mrs. Wushy said.

"Break a leg, Tiger," my papa whispered, as I stood up to go onstage.

I performed all my tricks perfectly. Then it was time for the grand finale. "And now, I need my assistant, Suzie, to come up and help me with this last trick. She will hold these two candlesticks."

Suzie came up onstage wearing a pink leotard and a cape trimmed in fur. "Ready?" I mouthed.

"Ready," she mouthed back, giving me a thumbs-up. "You can do this."

"Ladies and gentlemen, this trick is called the 'Ghost Wand.' I will place this wand in between these two candlesticks, and when I say the magic words, it will appear to move on its own. Watch closely. Abracadabra, Ghost of First-Grade Past, come and tap this wand."

Suzie pulled gently on the string, and the wand started tapping on the table. Oohs and aahs filled the room.

"Wow!" said Max. "How'd he do that?"

The kids and their grandparents jumped to their feet and gave me a standing ovation.

When I got back to my seat, Grammy Rose hugged me. "You were the star of the show!" she gushed.

"I'm really proud of you, Freddy," Papa Dave said, patting me on the back.

"Yeah," said Max. "You were really great."

"You mean you don't think I'm a loser?" I asked, astonished.

"No loser could do tricks like that, man."

I turned and smiled at Papa Dave, and he winked at me.

Now if he could just teach me how to make Suzie disappear. . . .

DEAR READER,

I have been a teacher for many years, and each year my class puts on a show for the parents. My students are very excited about performing, but some children are also scared to get up in front of so many people.

I remember a few years ago one little boy was so nervous, he threw up all over my shoes! To help my students stay calm, I tell them to just think of everyone in the audience in their underwear. That usually makes the kids laugh, and they forget about being nervous.

I bet you do some shows at your school, too. Have you ever been in a talent show? I'd love to hear about it. Just write to me at:

Ready, Freddy! Fun Stuff
c/o Scholastic Inc.
P. O. Box 711
New York, NY 10013-0711

I hope you have as much fun reading *Talent Show Scaredy-Pants* as I had writing it.

HAPPY READING!

Abby Klein

Freddy's Fun Pages

FREDDY'S SHARK JOURNAL

Sharks are talented, too! The mako shark is one of the fastest sharks. It can swim at a speed of more than 22 miles per hour.

The great white shark can eat about 11 tons of food a year.

Tiger sharks will eat anything. Fishermen have found many things in their stomachs, including a goat, glass bottles, and even pairs of shoes!

The brownbanded shark can live out of water for up to 12 hours.

The swell shark can swallow water or air and swell out its body to twice its normal size.

THE GHOST WAND TRICK

Do you believe in ghosts? Your friends will after they watch you perform this trick!

Note: For this trick, you will need a piece of clear nylon thread, two candles, and two candlesticks. You will also need a wand and an assistant.

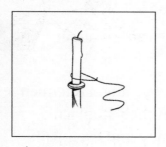

1. Tie a piece of clear nylon thread to one candle.

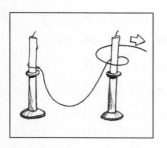

2. Loop the other end of the thread around another candle, but do not tie it. Make sure you leave an end of the thread hanging, so you can pull on it.

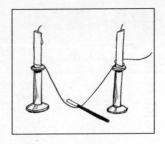

3. Place both candles in candlesticks on a table.

4. Place your wand on top of the thread between the two candlesticks.

5. When you are ready to perform, stand behind the table and say, "I believe there is a ghost in this room. When I say the magic words, the ghost will tap my wand on the table. Abracadabra, ghost, let us know you're here."

6. At this point your assistant will gently pull back and forth on the end of the thread you left hanging. This will make the wand tap the table.

Your friends won't believe their eyes!

PIN-THROUGH-
THE-THUMB TRICK

When you try this trick, your audience will
be amazed that you can stand the pain!

Note: Do not try this trick without adult supervision,
and never stick the pin into your real fingers!

1. Have an adult take a raw potato and cut it the
same size and shape as your thumb.

2. Hold the potato in your left
hand and bend your left thumb
into the palm of your hand,
hiding it. Cover your whole
hand with a handkerchief.

3. Then say, "Ladies and
gentlemen, watch closely. I
will now stick a pin through
my thumb." Then jam the pin
through the handkerchief right
into the potato (which looks
as if it is your thumb).

ROBBIE'S BEST JOKES

Here are some of the jokes Robbie
told at the talent show. Try telling some
to your friends!

Why do spiders do so well in computer class?
Because they love the Web.

Why didn't they let the wildcat in school?
Because they knew he was a cheetah.

What do you call two banana peels?
A pair of slippers.

Why was the rabbit so sad?
She was having a bad hare day.

Why was the car smelly?
It had too much gas.

What's big and white and lives on Mars?
A Martian-mallow.

Have you read all about Freddy?

Freddy will do anything to lose a tooth fast—even if it means getting in trouble with Mom!

Now that Freddy's found the best show-and-tell ever, how will he sneak his secret into school?

It's report time again, and Freddy's nocturnal research turns up some unexpected results!

Can Freddy beat out Max the bully to get the one open spot on the hockey team?

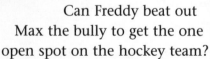